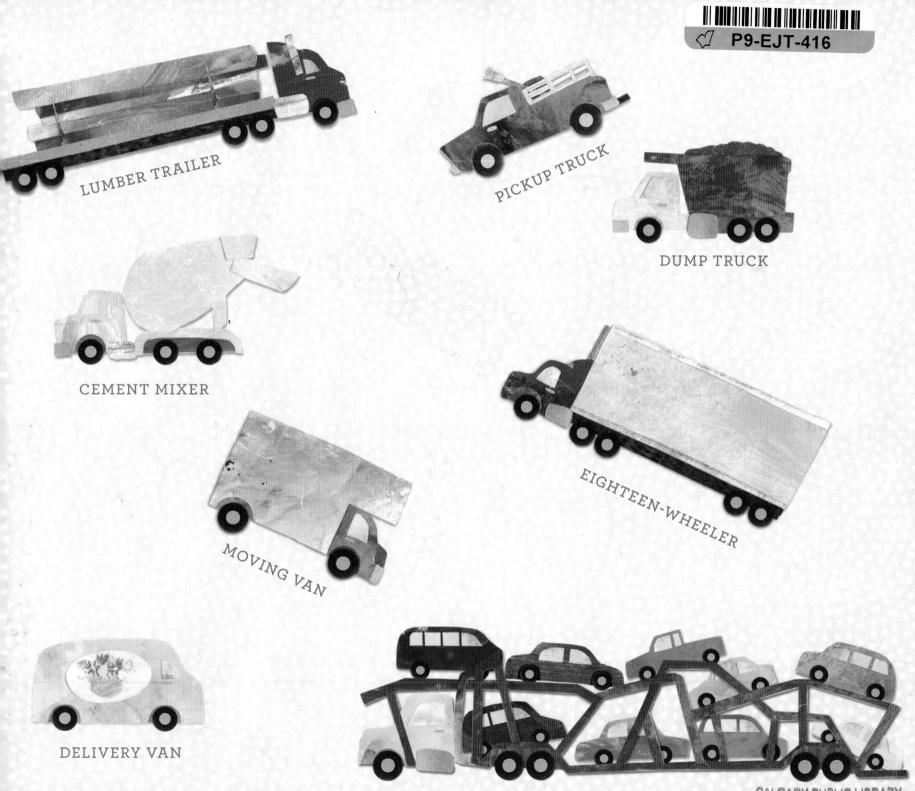

LUMBER TRAILER

PICKUP TRUCK

DUMP TRUCK

CEMENT MIXER

EIGHTEEN-WHEELER

MOVING VAN

DELIVERY VAN

AUTOMOBILE CARRIER

TRUCK STOP

Yes! we are OPEN

TRUCK STOP

Jim's DINER

FOOD FUEL

GAS

BY Anne Rockwell

ILLUSTRATED BY Melissa Iwai

TRUCK

EXPRESS LANE

DIESE

Viking

An Imprint of Penguin Group (USA) Inc.

Early each morning the sun isn't up
when we get busy at our truck stop, Mom and Dad and me.

Our truck stop is right beside the main highway heading north and south.

Every morning I squeeze the orange juice.
Dad cuts fries, sausages, and bacon, while Mom starts up the coffee.

Soon Uncle Marty turns on the lights in the service garage.
Another good morning has come!

I love it when the trucks start rolling in.
Their lights are bright in the dim, dark morning.
I know each and every one of the regulars that
comes to our truck stop.

I love how they come rumbling their wheels,
and with air brakes whooshing.
I love how the smell of diesel fills the air.

Eighteen-Wheeler is the first to arrive.
Sam, his driver, asks Uncle Marty to check all eighteen tires.

"Good morning!" he says to me.

"One coffee and bacon and eggs over easy!" says Mom.

"You bet!" says Sam.

Milk Tank and Maisie are next.
The big silver tank glows in the early pink dawn.

"One coffee and doughnuts coming up!" I call,
even before Maisie sits down at the counter.

Diligent Dan's Moving Van is next.

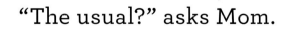

"The usual?" asks Mom.

"You bet—sausage and pancakes," says Dan.

"With plenty of syrup!" he adds.

"Where's Green Gus?" asks Eighteen-Wheeler's Sam.
"Yes, where's Green Gus?" ask Maisie and Dan.

Green Gus is the old green pickup
that rattles and clanks as it rolls—but always gets there.
Green Gus is always carting something here or there.
But where is Green Gus this morning?
No one has seen Green Gus today.

Not heading north.
Not heading south.

Flatbed pulls into the stop
with lots of loud cranking and whooshing—
carrying Digger to wherever needs digging.

Orange juice, black coffee, and a blueberry muffin
are what Flatbed's driver always wants.

Now our stop is filled with the good smells
of coffee brewing, bacon frying,
eggs sizzling sunny side up or over easy.

It's filled with the good sounds of morning, too.
Hard-working friends talking before they hit the road again,
some heading north, some heading south.

Pete and Priscilla's Tow Truck comes next.

"Have you seen Green Gus?" everyone asks, but Pete and Priscilla say no.

Suddenly Big Yellow Bus is here.
Big Yellow Bus has come for me as it always does
each weekday morning at the very same time.

I pick up my backpack and run to the bus.
It's time for me to go to school.

On the old blacktop road through the woods,
I suddenly see Green Gus
parked all alone on the side of the road with a very sad driver.

"Please call the truck stop to say I've found Green Gus!"
I ask the bus driver, and that's what she does.

Pete and Priscilla's Tow Truck is on the way. They'll tow Green Gus to our truck stop, where Uncle Marty will see what's wrong and fix Green Gus.

And the driver will have bacon and eggs sunny side up.

Then all the trucks can go on their way again,
including Green Gus.
Tomorrow I'll say good morning again,
when they come to our truck stop by the side of the highway,
where the big road heads north and south.

For Sullivan Wong Rockwell.—A.R.

*For all the truckers out there—the real Sams, Maisies, Dans, and others,
and the hard-working families who feed them.—M.I.*

VIKING
Published by the Penguin Group
Penguin Young Readers Group, 345 Hudson Street, New York, New York 10014, U.S.A.
Penguin Group (Canada), 90 Eglinton Avenue East, Suite 700, Toronto, Ontario, Canada M4P 2Y3 (a division of Pearson Penguin Canada Inc.)
Penguin Books Ltd, 80 Strand, London WC2R 0RL, England
Penguin Ireland, 25 St Stephen's Green, Dublin 2, Ireland (a division of Penguin Books Ltd)
Penguin Group (Australia), 250 Camberwell Road, Camberwell, Victoria 3124, Australia (a division of Pearson Australia Group Pty Ltd)
Penguin Books India Pvt Ltd, 11 Community Centre, Panchsheel Park, New Delhi – 110 017, India
Penguin Group (NZ), 67 Apollo Drive, Rosedale, Auckland 0632, New Zealand (a division of Pearson New Zealand Ltd.)
Penguin Books (South Africa) (Pty) Ltd, 24 Sturdee Avenue, Rosebank, Johannesburg 2196, South Africa

Penguin Books Ltd, Registered Offices: 80 Strand, London WC2R 0RL, England

First published in the United States of America by Viking, a division of Penguin Young Readers Group, 2013

3 5 7 9 10 8 6 4

Text copyright © Anne Rockwell, 2013
Illustrations copyright © Melissa Iwai, 2013
All rights reserved

LIBRARY OF CONGRESS CATALOGING-IN-PUBLICATION DATA
Rockwell, Anne F.
Truck stop / by Anne Rockwell ; illustrated by Melissa Iwai.
p. cm.
Summary: A boy and his parents prepare breakfast at their truck stop for drivers of eighteen-wheelers, tankers,
moving vans, and other vehicles, while Uncle Marty checks tires and makes repairs.
ISBN 978-0-670-06261-4 (hardcover)
[1. Truck stops—Fiction. 2. Motor vehicles—Fiction.] I. Iwai, Melissa, ill. II. Title.
PZ7.R5943Tru 2013   [E]—dc23   2012029239

Manufactured in China   Set in Archer   Book design by Nancy Brennan
This art was created using acrylic paint on board and watercolor paper, printed paper, colored paper, india ink, and digital manipulation.

ALWAYS LEARNING   PEARSON

MILK TANK

ICE CREAM TRUCK

FLATBED TRAILER

HORSE TRAILER

SCHOOL BUS

PICKUP TRUCK

TOW TRUCK

EIGHTEEN-WHEELER